For Winston

First American Edition 2015
Kane Miller, A Division of EDC Publishing

Text and illustrations copyright © 2014 Briony Stewart
First Published in Australia by University of Queensland Press
Translations rights arranged through Australian Licensing
Corporation

For information contact:
Kane Miller, A Division of EDC Publishing
P.O. Box 470663
Tulsa, OK 74147-0663

www.kanemiller.com
www.edcpub.com
www.usbornebooksandmore.com

Library of Congress Control Number: 2014939759
Printed and bound in China
5 6 7 8 9 10
ISBN: 978-1-61067-348-8

Here in the Garden

Briony Stewart

Kane Miller
A DIVISION OF EDC PUBLISHING

The wind is raking through the falling leaves
and I wish that you were here.

We'd skip over fallen branches
and search for leaves that
were the biggest and the brightest.

You'd help me plant seedlings in the garden as
we chatted and hummed like the birds.

My breath is making mist on the rain-dotted windows and I wish that you were here.

You'd sit beside me on the back steps
and watch the garden
turn deep and dark and green.

We'd dash over puddles and count how many things were pushing their way up through the ground.

The flowers are bursting and the bees are buzzing
and I wish that you were here.

We'd lie out on the grass
and trace the clouds drifting across the sky.

We'd search the garden for mysteries
cocoons and eggs and newly threaded webs.
You'd be proud of all the plants we'd grown.

The sun's streaming over my skin and under my feet
and I wish that you were here.

We'd slip under the shade of a tree
with cold drinks and ice cubes
as the sky burned every shade of blue.

You'd snooze and I'd sigh
until the sun sank down
and the crickets all came out to sing.

The garden's growing and changing,
and, when I wish that you were here …

I go outside and find you ...

In the memories,
in the garden,
in my heart.

The daughter of an artist and a biologist, Briony Stewart was always fascinated with the natural world and the magic in everyday life. After studying art and creative writing at university, she landed her dream job as a children's author and illustrator. Briony currently writes and illustrates in Perth, Western Australia, alongside her charming biologist husband, their pets and a wild, rambling backyard.